DINO-MIKE

AND THE
JURASSIC PORTAL

WRITTEN & ILLUSTRATED BY **FRANCO**

Raintree is an imprint of Capstone Global Library Limited,
a company incorporated in England and Wales having its
registered office at 7 Pilgrim Street, London, EC4V 6LB –
Registered company number: 6695582

www.raintree.co.uk
myorders@raintree.co.uk

ISBN 978-1-4062-9398-2 (paperback)
ISBN 978-1-4062-9403-3 (eBook)

18 17 16 15 14 10 9 8 7 6 5 4 3 2 1

British Library Cataloguing in Publication Data
A full catalogue record for this book is available from
the British Library.

Printed in China by Nordica
1214/CA21401920

CONTENTS

Young Mike Evans travels the world with his dino-hunting dad. From the Jurassic Coast in Dorset to the Liaoning Province in China, young Dino-Mike has been there, *dug* that!

While his dad is dusting fossils, Mike's busy refining his own dino skills – only he's out discovering the real thing. A live T. rex egg! A portal to the Jurassic period!! An undersea dinosaur sanctuary!!!

Prepare yourself for another wild and wacky Dino-Mike adventure, one which nobody will ever believe...

Chapter 1
TIME WARP

"I'm GLOWING!" Mike screamed.

He was indeed glowing ... and falling! FAST! Mike wasn't sure where he'd eventually land, but that thought didn't make him panic. He was more concerned about the strange radioactive glow. Dr Broome had told him that this might happen, but it still didn't seem safe.

Glowing in the dark can't be good for you. It's just not normal, Mike worried. *I may never get a good night's sleep again!*

Suddenly, there was a rush of air, and then **THUD!** Dino-Mike hit the ground.

"Uhhh..." Mike groaned in pain.

A moment later, Dino-Mike lifted his head and looked down at his hands. They were still glowing!

"How do I switch this off?" Mike exclaimed. He knew any nearby animals would be attracted to the strange light.

Mike stood and brushed the dirt off of his Dino Jacket. The hi-tech hoodie – the best-ever present from his dad – had helped him once again. The Dino Jacket's specially designed fabric had cushioned his fall and saved him from breaking bones ... or worse.

Mike's glowing skin soon returned to normal, but his problems had just begun.

Mike needed to find his dino-hunting sidekick, Shannon. He'd agreed to travel back in time because her mad-scientist father, Dr Broome, needed help.

Dino-Mike reached inside his hoodie and pulled out a small gadget. The hi-tech device looked like a TV remote control. In fact, it *was* a TV remote control! Dr Broome had transformed the device into Mike's life support, which he called a Return Remote.

When Mike had located Shannon, he needed to return to this spot and click the device's rewind button. That would return them both to the present day.

Priority number one, Mike thought,
find Shannon.

Mike scanned his surroundings.
He still didn't know where he was or
even which time period he was in.
However, being the son of a famous
palaeontologist, Dino-Mike did know a
lot about dinosaurs and their habitats.

Mike observed his surroundings. "The late Jurassic," he concluded. "Or maybe the early Cretaceous period. There's only one way to know for sure –"

CRUNNNNNNNNNNNNNCH!

Suddenly, Dino-Mike heard a loud crunching noise in the nearby forest. Whatever was behind those trees would be a clue to his location. But Mike wasn't sure he wanted to find out what was making that noise.

Dino-Mike followed a nearby trail away from the sound. Soon, he stopped and pulled a journal from the inside pocket of his Dino Jacket.

The journal didn't belong to him. It belonged to his worst enemy...

"Jurassic Jeff," Mike growled.

Jurassic Jeff had one evil goal: to repopulate present-day Earth with dinosaurs. He'd stop at nothing to accomplish this fearsome feat.

Oh, and he just happened to be Shannon's big brother! Crazy, isn't it?

On his last big adventure, Dino-Mike managed to secure Jeff's journal. Mike hoped it would reveal Jeff's secret plans.

Leafing through the journal, Mike found maps. Landmarks on one map seemed to match Mike's location!

FWOOOOSH!

A sudden wind flipped the pages of the journal.

FWOOOOSH!

The wind blew again, hot and humid like the breath of a...

Dino-Mike plunged the journal into his pocket and spun around. He was nose to horn with an angry dinosaur.

"Triceratops!" Mike exclaimed.

Chapter 2
CHARGE!

"A triple threat!" Mike screamed.

Mike quickly turned and sprinted away from the three-horned beast. The triceratops was hot on his trail.

Mike knew he could never outrun a triceratops. His in-depth knowledge of dinos meant that Mike knew they could run like rhinos – thirty miles an hour!

Thinking quickly, Mike stopped and spun towards the triceratops. He grabbed his hood and flipped it onto his head.

"DINO-MIKE!" he screamed.

ROOOOAAAAAAAARRRRR!

The sound of a T. rex's roar blasted from speakers inside his Dino Jacket.

That should scare him, thought Mike.

The beast grunted and snorted and his eyes turned red with rage.

"Uh-oh," said Mike. In his panic, he'd forgotten that triceratops, unlike most dinosaurs, often defended themselves from T. rex attacks.

The triceratops thrashed, snorted again and kicked up dirt. Then the beast charged at Dino-Mike like a raging bull.

"Move!" shouted a nearby voice.

A split-second later, someone tackled Mike out of the triceratops's path. He hit the ground with another **THUD!**

"Ugh," Mike said, picking himself up off the ground. "What are you doing?"

"You can thank me later," said the redheaded girl standing next to him.

"SHANNON!" Mike exclaimed, recognizing his dino-hunting sidekick. "I'm so glad to see you –"

"Less talk," Shannon interrupted, "more running!"

SMASH! CRASH!

The angry triceratops had turned around. It was smashing and crashing through the trees towards the duo.

"Follow me!" cried Shannon. She turned and headed straight into a mess of thick plants and vines.

"We'll never outrun him in here," shouted Mike.

"We don't need to," Shannon replied.

Breaking through the vines, Dino-Mike spotted the edge of a cliff only a metre or two away. The cliff dropped more than thirty metres to a valley below!

"We're trapped!" Mike shouted at Shannon as the triceratops edged them closer to the cliff. "Why did you lead us here?"

Shannon grabbed Mike's wrist. "Sorry," she explained, "didn't have time to think it through!"

Then Shannon leapt off the cliff, pulling Dino-Mike along with her.

"AHH!" Mike screamed as they plummeted towards the ground below.

Chapter 3

FREE FALL

"Hey!" screamed Mike. "I thought you were my dino-hunting sidekick. I should know about big decisions, like jumping off of cliffs!"

"You're right," said Shannon. "From now on, I'll tell you everything."

As they fell, Shannon grabbed the drawstrings of Dino-Mike's hoodie.

"Just so you know," she shouted at Mike, "I'm going to pull these."

"Wait!" shouted Dino-Mike.

But Shannon had already pulled the strings. As she did, a pair of wings sprouted from under Mike's arms!

FWOOSH! For a moment, Mike and Shannon glided above the ground.

"How did you know my Dino Jacket had wings?" Mike asked Shannon.

"Your hoodie has all kinds of dinosaur powers," Shannon replied. "I just assumed it had a pterodactyl mode."

"Did you also assume I could fly it?" asked Dino-Mike.

Mike flapped his wings frantically, and soon the duo was plummeting towards the ground again.

Just then, an alarm sounded, and the Dino Jacket puffed up like a balloon!

BEEP! BEEP! BEEP!

"What's that noise?" asked Shannon.

"I don't know," Mike replied. "The Dino Jacket must have some sort of emergency safety mode!"

Dino-Mike and Shannon floated slowly towards the valley below. When they hit the ground, the jacket bounced several times like a giant basketball.

Finally they came to a stop. The Dino Jacket quickly deflated back to its original size and shape.

"So, what exactly are you doing here?" Shannon asked, ignoring the fact that they'd almost died.

"Your father sent me to find you," replied Mike.

"My father?" asked Shannon. "Did he give you a Return Remote?"

"Yes," said Mike, reaching into his Dino Jacket and revealing the hi-tech device. "Here it is."

"OH MY GOSH! Do you know what this means?" Shannon exclaimed.

"It means we can get out of here," answered Dino-Mike. He grabbed Shannon's arm and started pulling her along a nearby trail.

"Wait!" said Shannon. "We can't. Not yet, anyway."

"Why not?" asked Mike, puzzled.

Shannon hesitated and then said, "First of all, we need to find Jeff."

Dino-Mike gritted his teeth, and his face turned redder than a tomato.

"JURASSIC JEFF!" Mike shouted, sweat and steam rising from his forehead. "My. Worst. Enemy."

"Don't forget, Mike," said Shannon, "he's also my brother."

"A real brother wouldn't kidnap his sister and drag her to the Jurassic Age!" Mike responded.

"To start with," Shannon began, "this isn't the Jurassic Age. It's the Cretaceous period. Any dino-hunter would know that!"

"D'oh!" Mike exclaimed.

"Secondly," Shannon continued, "Jeff didn't kidnap me. I chose to come back in time with him."

"Are you joking?" said Mike.

"You're not going to believe me, Mike, but we have a much bigger problem than my brother!" Shannon explained.

"What could possibly be worse than Jurassic Jeff?" shouted Mike.

"MUM!" Shannon exclaimed.

"What are you talking about?" Mike demanded.

"For years, Jeff has tried to bring a dinosaur back to the present day," Shannon explained. "But MUM is trying to bring back thousands!"

"THOUSANDS!" Mike repeated.

"That's what I've been trying to tell you," said Shannon. "Jeff might be evil minded, but MUM is an evil mastermind."

"But why?" asked Dino-Mike.

"She's just programmed that way, I suppose," Shannon said.

"How can we stop her?" asked Mike.

"You're not going to like my answer," Shannon began. "But we're going to have to work with Jurassic Jeff!"

"Uh-uh," said Mike, shaking his head.

"Come on, Mike," Shannon pleaded. "It could be our only chance. Jurassic Jeff's the only one who knows how to push MUM's buttons."

"How can we trust him?" asked Dino-Mike. He thought back to Jeff's past adventures. Just weeks ago, the evil teenager had released a T. rex onto the streets of New York City! That event could have ended in disaster.

"I can't lie to you," replied Shannon. "Jeff hasn't changed. But he does understand that MUM's plan goes too far. Not even he'll be safe from thousands of dinosaurs."

"Maybe you're right," said Mike.

"Anyway," Shannon continued, "do we have any other choice? At this moment, Jeff is the lesser of two evils. What do you say? Are you ready to take a leap of faith with me, old pal?"

"Um, haven't I already done that?" Mike replied, pointing to the nearby cliff.

The duo laughed.

Then Mike stepped towards Shannon and extended his hand.

"Okay," he said. "We'll work with Jeff until your mum is captured … but don't ask me to like it."

Shannon smiled and then reached out and shook Dino-Mike's hand.

"It's a deal!" she said.

"DINO-MIKE!" they both exclaimed.

Chapter 4

FAMILY TREE

Following Jurassic Jeff's journal,
Dino-Mike and Shannon made their way
across the narrow valley. Finally, they
reached a small, dense forest.

"Shh," Shannon shushed Mike. "Be
quiet and pay attention!" She kneeled
down and studied a large footprint in
the mud.

"A dinosaur?" asked Mike.

Dino-Mike stepped forwards to take a closer look. "Which species?" he wondered. "Diplodocus? Pentaceratops?"

Shannon started to giggle.

"What is it?" questioned Mike. "Do you know what kind of track that is?"

WHUMP!

Mike was suddenly tackled to the ground.

"A Jurassic Jeff track!" Shannon said, letting out a laugh.

Mike tried to move, but Jurassic Jeff had pinned him to the ground. "Get off of me!" shouted Dino-Mike, struggling to get free.

Finally Jeff stood and turned to Shannon. "What is he doing here?"

"Trying to help you!" said Dino-Mike, standing and dusting off his Dino Jacket.

"What are you talking about?" asked Jeff. "How are *you* going to help *me*?!"

"It's true," Shannon explained to her brother. "Dad sent him to find us."

"Again, what are you talking about?" asked Jeff. "How did Dad send him to the exact same place as us? He must have worked out how to time target!"

"He sent me because he thought you had kidnapped Shannon," said Mike.

"Why would he think that?" said Jeff.

"Well," said Shannon, "you haven't exactly been trustworthy in the past."

"Oh," said Jeff. "When you put it that way, I suppose I might have thought that too. But still, it says a lot that Dad sent him. Means he really trusts you, Mike."

Dino-Mike took the compliment. Jeff had given him a lot of trouble in the past (he was Mike's worst enemy, after all!), but it seemed as though he wanted to be a better person.

"Thanks," Mike said.

Shannon spoke up again. "Dad doesn't know about MUM."

"Makes sense," said Jeff. "If he did, he probably wouldn't have sent Mike."

How bad can their mother be? thought Mike. He knew he'd probably find out soon enough!

Jeff turned to go back into the forest and started walking down a narrow path.

"If we're going to track MUM, we better get going!" he said, leading the way. "Oh, and welcome to the expedition, Mike. Don't get your hopes up about ever returning home."

"Thanks," said Mike. He knew Jeff's kindness wouldn't last long.

Chapter 5
CAVE MUM

A while later, the group peered at the entrance of a cave.

"Do you think MUM's in there?" asked Shannon.

They had travelled for an hour through dense leaves, vines and branches. It was the hardest trek through any stretch of forest Dino-Mike had ever made.

"If she isn't, she will be soon." Jeff moved behind a nearby tree to get a better look at the cave. "The equipment she needs is stored in that cave."

"Unless she's already been here and is back out gathering more herds of dinosaurs," Shannon suggested.

"Um…" Mike interrupted. "Not that I don't know what you're talking about, but what are you talking about?!"

"In case you haven't noticed, Jeff is very tech savvy. He has developed some equipment that will enhance the portal process," explained Shannon.

"What does that mean?" asked Mike.

"It means that I think I have worked out a way of making the time portal operate on a large scale," said Jeff, still trying to get a better look into the cave.

"Large scale," repeated Mike. "Does he mean…?"

"If MUM accesses the portal with the equipment Jeff has developed, she might be able to transport a whole herd of dinosaurs in one go," confirmed Shannon.

"That was before I, you know, became good," Jeff reminded them. "The last T. rex I brought back was my phase-one experiment. I knew that if I could transport one dinosaur directly to a site, I had the ability to transport an entire herd at once."

"So it's not just a possibility. If your mum gets that equipment she would be able to bring thousands of dinosaurs to the present day?" asked Mike.

"Yes," said Jeff. "That's right."

"Oh my goodness!" exclaimed Mike.

Mike looked at Shannon. It was up to them to think of a plan. Mike thought carefully about the situation.

If Jeff and Shannon's mum needed that equipment, the simplest solution would be to stop her from using it. Mike looked at the cave entrance. Above the mouth of the cave was a pile of rocks that must have tumbled down from further up the hillside. There was a tree blocking their path. Without the tree, the rocks could fall and possibly block the opening to the cave.

Mike started
climbing a tree faster
than a monkey.

FWIP! FWIP!

Raptor claws in
Mike's sleeves dug into
the bark of the tree,
making his climb
quite easy.

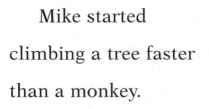

Before Shannon
could shout out for him
to stop, he was already
at the top of the tree.

Swinging from tree to tree, Mike made it to the space just above the cave entrance. Then suddenly, Mike froze.

In front of him was a family of triceratops – a mother and two little ones. Based on his last encounter, Dino-Mike wasn't particularly excited to see them!

The mother was huge, as you would expect a dinosaur to be. The young triceratops were roughly the size of rhinoceroses, which meant they were still a lot bigger than Dino-Mike. Like all good campers, Mike knew not to mess with a mother and her cubs.

That gave Dino-Mike an idea!

Dino-Mike approached the grazing triceratops cautiously. At first, the family of triceratops completely ignored him. Obviously, these triceratops were not even remotely related to the triceratops he had met at the landing point, or they would have chased him the minute he appeared above the cave.

Mike stood tall and pulled on the drawstrings of his hoodie. Two streams of water blasted out of the drawstring holes and hit the mother triceratops on the bottom!

SPA-LOOOOOOOOOSH!

The mother triceratops reacted as
if a swarm of bees, rather than a cool
stream of water, had hit her. She
spotted Mike and let out
a **ROOOOAR!**

The triceratops turned towards him and, along with her babies, started running straight towards Mike.

Okay, maybe this was a mistake, thought Mike.

Dino-Mike ran for the rocks and trees. He had to time this just right. Mike stepped up onto the rocks, ran over them while trying not to lose his footing, and leapt, only just missing the tree that was holding up the rocks above the cave.

As he jumped, Mike looked back to see if his plan had worked. Sure enough, the mother triceratops had smashed into the tree, splintering it into pieces.

In doing so, the rocks that were being held back started to give way. The triceratops mum and her babies scrambled off the large pile of rocks to safety before the rocks fell over the cliff.

Mike watched all this happen as his Dino Jacket came to his rescue once more. He heard the distinct sound of air rushing through the jacket's vents. The jacket inflated to the size of a large balloon, and Mike gently floated to the tree line where Shannon and Jeff waited.

As he landed, the large rocks that had been dislodged began crashing down and covering the entrance to the cave.

Jeff and Shannon came out from behind the trees. Mike smiled as he surveyed his handiwork.

"See? It's all sorted," said Mike as his jacket deflated back to normal size. "Your mum is trapped in there. Now we can go back to the future, tell your dad, and bring back some help."

"I don't know," said Jeff. "That's not going to hold MUM for long."

"I think you're right," said Shannon. "And now MUM knows we're here!"

Mike was in total disbelief. "What is the matter with you two? Your mother is never going to get out of there without help. Those rocks weigh a ton!"

"My mother?" asked Jeff.

"What makes you think our mother is in the cave?" asked Shannon.

"Because you said your mum was in there," Mike screamed.

"No. We said *MUM* was in there," explained Jeff.

"What's the difference?" asked Mike.

Suddenly, there was a loud **CRACK!**

The group turned just in time to see the pile of rocks covering the entrance to the cave explode outwards.

SMAAASSSSSSSSSSSH!!!

A large mechanical robot emerged from the cave. It loomed over the group. Mike couldn't believe his eyes. The robot was lifting the largest boulder – the one that Mike couldn't shift at the top of the ridge – over its head.

Shannon said, *"That's* MUM!"

Chapter 6
ROCK AND ROLL

"Your mum's a ROBOT?!" asked Mike, still confused.

The robot – which did not look anything like a mum – lifted another boulder over its head. Then the mechanical menace tossed the huge rock to the ground with all its might.

WHAM-O!

Dino-Mike gulped in fright.

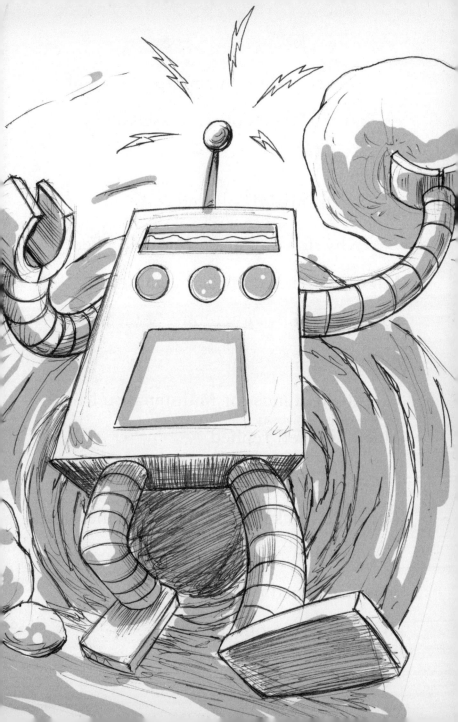

"No! That's not our mother!" Shannon explained. "Our mother passed away when we were young."

"That's MUM!" offered Jeff.

"Why do you have a MUM?" asked Mike, realizing that the question sounded totally ridiculous. "I mean, a robot called MUM?"

"MUM stands for Maintenance Utility Machine," Jeff replied.

"It was a maintenance robot our dad retrofitted to keep an eye on us whenever we visited in the past," said Shannon as they continued to watch the robot work to clear itself from the rubble.

"You mean your dad made you a robot nanny that would protect you in case you were attacked by a T. rex?" asked Dino-Mike.

"Something like that. But me being me, I reprogrammed it," offered Jeff.

"To help you bring dinosaurs to the future?" asked Mike. Things were starting to make sense now.

"I had a one-track mind when it came to dinosaurs," said Jeff. "I programmed MUM to bring back one dinosaur, but somehow the program got stuck on repeat. The robot won't stop now until it brings all of them back."

"Then shut it down!" Mike shouted.

"I can't. I overrode the failsafe switch, so no one could turn it off. It won't stop until it accomplishes its task, until present-day Earth is overrun by dinosaurs," said Jeff, starting to panic.

"Then we need to destroy it!" screamed Mike.

THUD!

A large boulder landed just inches away from the trio.

"That won't be easy!" said Shannon.

"It's superstrong and programmed to do two things," Jeff started. "Bring dinosaurs back to our time and –"

Shannon pushed both her brother
and Mike down to the ground as another
rock landed, only just missing them.

WHAM!

From the ground, they watched as
the MUM robot grabbed
another rock and
hoisted the boulder
over its head.

"What's the second thing?" asked Mike, very worried about what the answer might be.

"Stop anyone who's trying to prevent it from bringing dinosaurs to our time," said Jeff.

They were stuck. All three of them were on the ground as the MUM robot approached. There was no way of escaping.

MUM was going to drop the rock right on top of them.

Mike held his breath. "Could this be the end of Dino-Mike?" he muttered.

Chapter 7

ROCK AND SOCK 'EM

CLANG!

It was the sudden and horrible sound of metal being hit by something big. The crunching and scraping sound of the metal echoed throughout the forest.

They'd been saved! Mike watched as the triceratops smashed into the side of MUM. The robot toppled over.

The boulder it was holding toppled with it. The mother triceratops had made her way down the ridge with her babies. Apparently still angry with Mike for squirting her with water, she rammed into the side of the MUM robot.

Without thinking, Mike jumped up and let out a "HOORAY!" He was so relieved not to be crushed under a rock hurled by a robot. The sound of his rejoicing caught the attention of the triceratops. It turned towards him, Shannon and Jeff.

"Uh-oh," said Shannon. "I don't think you should have done that."

The two small triceratops ran towards them. Luckily, the mother triceratops turned its attention back to MUM.

"We just swapped being squashed by a rock for being trampled by dinosaurs!" said Jeff. "RUN!"

Mike, Shannon and Jeff were just steps ahead of the charging triceratops!

"What else do you have in that Dino Jacket of yours, Mike?" asked Shannon.

Mike turned as Jeff and Shannon kept running. As he turned, he flipped his hood over his head. The T. rex eyes lit up like fireworks, flooding the area with light and blinding the triceratops.

The T. rex roar bellowed from the speakers of the hoodie. The two triceratops were caught by surprise. Their thundering footsteps suddenly changed to scrambling steps as they tried to get out of the way.

The roar was deafening and, although it scared away the younger triceratops, it also attracted attention Mike didn't want. After his T. rex roar faded, Mike heard a different kind of pounding.

He looked up to see MUM heading straight towards him. The robot was almost on top of him. The only thing he could think to do as the robot reached for him was to jump up in the air.

His jacket quickly ballooned out like a round ball. MUM grabbed him in his puffy-jacket state, lifted him higher into the air, and squeezed.

It worked! Mike felt uncomfortable as MUM squeezed, but at least he wasn't getting crushed. Unfortunately, the squeezing caused the Return Remote to pop out of his jacket. Mike could only look on helplessly as it fell.

He saw something else, though. The mother triceratops was back and headed straight towards MUM.

As it charged, it crushed the Return Remote under its foot!

SMASH!

The triceratops smashed its horned head into the body of the robot. The clash knocked Mike loose from the robot's grip. He floated gently back to the ground.

As his jacket deflated, Jeff and Shannon ran up to him. They helped move Dino-Mike out of the way of the fighting robot and dinosaur.

"The Return Remote!" shouted Mike, pointing at the shattered device.

"What are we going to do?" asked Shannon.

"MUM's the answer," said Jeff. "Its internal return function is the only way for us to get back!"

"So, let me get this right," Mike began. "We need to destroy the robot in order to save present-day Earth. But, if we destroy the robot, we're trapped here forever?!"

"Correct," answered Jurassic Jeff.

"That is NOT good," said Mike.

Meanwhile, MUM had given its full attention to the triceratops. It clamped one hand down on the main horn of the dinosaur. This stopped the dinosaur from doing any more damage.

In fact, it stopped the dinosaur from doing anything at all. By holding on to its horn, MUM was able to drag the triceratops around like a dog on a lead.

"Uh-oh," said Jeff.

They all knew that having the dinosaur under control meant that MUM would be coming after them next.

"What shall we do, Jeff?" asked Shannon.

"How should I know? I didn't build it!" said Jeff.

Mike couldn't think of a way out either. He decided to take action, still not entirely sure of what he was going to do.

He started running at the robot. As he reached the robot's legs, Mike reached out his arms as if to climb it like he would a tree. Sure enough, his raptor claws sprung out of his sleeves. **FWIP! FWIP!**

Mike used the claws to dig into the robot's metal legs. He started to climb.

"What are you doing?" said Shannon.

"Jeff, is the central processor in the head?" yelled down Mike.

"Yes, but..." replied Jeff, but then he thought about Mike's question. "If we could somehow separate MUM's head from the rest of the body, it would be like unplugging it. MUM would just shut down, and we could probably still use the internal Return Remote housed in its body to get us home!"

They watched helplessly as Mike scrambled to the top of MUM. He held on tightly and positioned himself behind MUM's head.

The robot released the triceratops and started swatting at Mike like a fly. Dino-Mike zigged and zagged, avoiding the mechanical menace's metal arms. Mike knew he didn't have much time.

At the same time, Shannon searched for a way to stop the triceratops and her babies. Suddenly, she noticed all of the vines that had wrapped themselves around the tall trees.

"I've got an idea! Help me gather these vines!" she shouted over to Jeff.

MUM spotted Shannon and Jeff and began to move towards them. Mike couldn't let the robot follow them. He took off his Dino Jacket and wrapped it around the robot's head, blinding it.

Mike needed to shut down the robot, but to do that he would have to separate its head from its body.

He looked in the hood of his Dino Jacket. The inside of the hoodie was lined with an array of buttons. Mike quickly found the button he needed.

Mike pushed the button, and the jacket began to inflate to the size of a large balloon. Because the jacket was wrapped around the robot's head, it started to lift the whole robot off of the ground.

Mike held on tightly.

Then MUM suddenly stopped with a jerk. Jeff and Shannon had tied the robot to the ground with vines!

With a loud **CREAK!**, the robot's head started separating from its body.

MUM's head, wrapped in the Dino Jacket, lifted into the air along with a string of wires and metal from the inside of the robot. When the last of the wiring ripped from the body of the robot, the forest immediately fell quiet.

"It worked!" shouted Dino-Mike.

Just then, Mike looked down to see Jeff and Shannon desperately trying to get his attention. Something was wrong. They were pointing above him.

Dino-Mike looked up and couldn't believe it. His Dino Jacket, zipped up around the head of the robot, was shooting into the air like a rocket!

Mike's mouth dropped open with shock as he watched it. The jacket must have calculated for the entire weight of the robot, but when the head was dislodged, it had not made any corrections. It thought it was still carrying the entire robot body.

Mike watched as the jacket and the robot head continued up into the sky and then disappeared from sight.

Dino-Mike didn't have time to be cross. The headless robot swayed backwards and forwards, ready to tip at any moment.

"TIMBER!" cried Dino-Mike, holding tightly to the falling robot.

CRAAAAASSHHHH!!!

The MUM robot hit the ground, and the ground shook like a violent earthquake. A cloud of thick dust rose into the air.

Shannon and Jeff shielded their eyes. They couldn't see their friend through the dust and debris.

Then a figure emerged from the dust cloud, coughing and spitting. "Looks like we scared away the triceratops," said Mike, dusting himself off.

"DINO-MIKE!" Shannon and Jeff exclaimed.

Chapter 8

STUCK

"We're stuck here," said Jeff as he climbed down from the robot body.

Jeff explained how the Return Remote components had been ripped out of the body when the head was separated. Somewhere in that mess of spaghetti wire Mike watched float away was their ticket home.

"At the rate that thing was going, the head probably shot right into outer space," finished Jeff as his boots hit the ground.

"I can't believe my Dino Jacket is gone," said Mike. "It was a present from my dad, and now ... it's lost forever."

Shannon put her hand on Mike's shoulder to comfort him. "You saved our lives. You're a hero," said Shannon.

She's right, thought Mike. *As long as we're okay, the jacket doesn't matter.*

With the robot destroyed, there was little hope of getting back home. Mike would not be defeated – he started thinking aloud.

"We could wait for your dad to send someone back for us!" said Mike.

"Yes, but that could take years," said Shannon. "Time travel is never exact, precisely because you're dealing with time. Dad will send someone back, but for us to see them arrive, it could be minutes or years or ... never."

"The only way we can get back is with something that has already travelled forwards in time through the portal," explained Jeff.

"Easy!" said Mike. "You two have already done that."

"It's not that easy," said Jeff. "For some reason it doesn't work with people. That's why we need the Return Remotes. My dad was the one who discovered how time travel works. I'm quite good with computers and gadgets, but time travel is just out of my league."

"When Dad first developed all this, he tried lots of different things. He sent objects backwards and forwards through time to see what worked and what didn't before deciding it was safe enough to try it on a human being ... himself."

"What kind of things?" asked Mike.

"He told us he tried everything: tools, food, plants and goldfish. You name it, he probably sent it here," said Shannon.

"Great! We just need to find one of those things, and we're good to go, aren't we?" said a hopeful Mike.

"No. Everything he sent, he brought back again. He didn't want to accidentally leave something from our time that someone would eventually discover through the ages," said Jeff.

"So we're stuck millions of years in the past with a deranged MUM robot and dinosaurs at every turn," shouted Mike, defeated.

Everyone fell silent. Mike let out a sigh and sat down on the nearest rock. He would never see his dad again.

It's funny, Mike thought. *Dad would love this place.*

Dino-Mike stared at the ground. There were reminders all around that dinosaurs roamed the planet freely. He immediately recognized a fresh dinosaur footprint on the ground in front of him.

It was the footprint of a fully grown T. rex! It reminded him of the one his father and a team of palaeontologists had unearthed just a few months earlier.

That was the day he had met Shannon.

"Wait a minute!" said Mike, standing up and grabbing Shannon by the shoulders. "The T. rex! *Our* T. rex – the one we named Samantha! Did you bring her here!"

Shannon's eyes doubled in size.

"Yes!" she said.

Jeff knew exactly what they were talking about. "You and Dad brought her back here?" he asked Shannon.

"Yes!" said Shannon. She smiled for a moment but then stopped. "But how are we going to find her?"

Mike pulled out a journal from his back pocket. "With this!"

"My journal!" said Jeff. "Where did you find that?"

"In your room on the *Atlantica* submarine," replied Mike slowly, thinking Jeff was going to be angry that he had looked through his things.

Jeff moved closer to Mike. For a split second, Mike thought Jeff was going to attack him. But Jeff hugged him instead. Mike was shocked.

"Mike!" said Jeff, continuing the hug. "I am so happy that you brought my journal along!"

Chapter 9
OLD FRIENDS

Mike was getting tired of sneaking around. But if they could pull this off, they would all be able to go home.

They were close to the landing site, next to the nest of a mother T. rex and her babies. This wasn't just any T. rex, either. It was Samantha. Mike had run into her on earlier dino adventures!

Mike, Shannon and Jeff looked at
the T. rex and her four babies, which
had grown a couple of feet since the
last time Mike saw them. They were
frolicking around her like a litter of new
puppies.

Because the babies had been born in New York, only the mother T. rex had gone forwards in time. That meant that only she could trigger the portal. The plan was to take one of the babies and lure the mother to the landing site in the hope that she would activate the portal.

The plan was easy. It was very dangerous – but simple.

"I'm not too sure about this," said Shannon.

"Me neither. But it's our only chance to get back, other than hoping we will get rescued. I think it's a risk we should take." whispered Jeff.

"It's dangerous," said Shannon.

"This won't be the first time today that we've done something dangerous," whispered Mike.

Shannon gave him a look that said both: "Yes, you're right" and "I can't believe this is about to happen."

"Okay," she said finally. "How are we going to do this?"

"Without the Dino Jacket, it's going to be difficult. If two of us distract the mother and one of us swoops in and grabs a baby, with any luck she'll chase us. We can lead her back to the landing site," said Mike.

"I'm not sure that calling them babies is appropriate. Those things are over a metre long now," said Jeff.

"Because Jeff and I have the most experience with larger dinosaurs, we'll attract the mother's attention. You get in and try to attract the attention of one of the babies," said Shannon.

"I really wish we had a can of Dad's knockout spray," said Jeff.

Mike smiled as he remembered the minty taste of the green knockout spray. He wished they had a can too. *It would make things so much easier,* he thought.

Mike lifted the makeshift lead they had made out of vines for one of the baby T. rex. He looked at Shannon and Jeff. They nodded at each other and started putting their plan into action.

Mike waited for a few minutes as Shannon and Jeff moved through the trees. Then he made his way to the

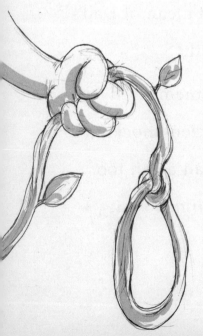

opposite end of the open field where the T. rex were. He waited for the right time.

From the other side of the field he heard Jeff's voice. "Hey, you big old T. rex!"

BOOOOM! BOOOOM!

Mike could hear the booming footsteps of the mother T. rex as she moved away. Mike looked out and saw Jeff and Shannon waving to try to attract the dinosaur's attention.

"Come on! We're over here! Chase us!" Shannon called out.

The T. rex moved in their direction. Jeff and Shannon didn't wait any longer and they both started running into the forest.

Mike jumped out from the trees and sprinted straight towards one of the baby T. rex.

Dino-Mike chose the closest one, slipped the lead around its neck and immediately started to run.

"I've got one! I've got one!" he shouted, so that Jeff and Shannon could hear him and make their way to the landing site.

Suddenly Mike was jerked back, and he almost fell as the T. rex stood fast. Mike quickly got back to his feet and tugged the lead. The T. rex wouldn't budge.

Now it had caught the attention of the other three baby T. rex. Mike was pulling with all his might, but the T. rex would not move.

The four T. rex began playing and frolicking with each other. One of them was even chewing the makeshift lead.

"No," whispered Mike. He didn't have time for this.

If he couldn't get one of these dinosaurs to the landing site, they would never get out of there. Or worse, the mother T. rex would catch up with Jeff and Shannon. Or even worse than that –

ROOOOOARRRRRRRRR!

The mother T. rex would give up chasing Shannon and Jeff and come back and check on her babies.

Mike was trapped.

He was caught between the mother T. rex and her four babies with nowhere to run. There was too much open field to try to reach the safety of any trees. This was not good.

Behind the lumbering mother T. rex, Mike could see Shannon and Jeff emerge from the forest. They wouldn't be able to do anything to help him.

The mother came closer and closer until Mike could feel hot breath shoot from her nostrils. Mike was frozen with fear until the mother T. rex nudged him ever so gently with the tip of her snout.

Mike didn't understand what was happening. The mother nudged him again, but a bit harder this time as she snorted. Now the baby T. rex joined in. They were all over Mike, carefully pulling at his clothes and pushing him this way and that.

Dino-Mike realized that they were playing with him. They were treating him as if he was one of the family.

Jeff and Shannon came closer but kept enough distance so that the mother did not react.

"W-what's happening?" asked Mike.

"How cute," said Shannon. "They must remember you from before. They probably imprinted on you. You were the first thing they had contact with, so they feel close to you."

"We've seen this happen before, dinosaurs becoming friendly with their keepers," said Jeff.

"I think they like you," said Shannon, giggling a bit.

"What do we do now?" asked Jeff.

Mike looked at the lead dangling from the neck of one of the baby dinosaurs and slowly reached for it. Reaching it without incident, he started to lead the dinosaur.

"Follow me, but keep your distance," he said to Shannon and Jeff.

Sure enough, the entire family went with him. They would run ahead or bump Mike playfully through the course of the entire walk. The mother T. rex followed right on their heels.

Mike led them all the way to the landing site. Within feet of the spot where Mike landed, the mother T. rex stopped. She wouldn't go any further.

"What's the matter with her? Why did she stop?" asked Mike.

"She remembers this spot," said Jeff. "She remembers what it was like to go through the time portal the first time, and she didn't like it."

"Well, what do we do now?" asked Shannon.

Mike looked behind him and saw the four baby T. rex being their usual playful selves, but they were glowing!

"THEY'RE GLOWING!" said Mike.

Dino-Mike knew what this meant. It meant that they were – but how? They didn't go forwards in time ... because they hadn't hatched.

"They hadn't hatched, but technically they did go forwards! They were carried by their mother! It's basic biology!" Mike exclaimed.

"That's right! They're activating the time portal!" said Jeff.

"They're getting glowier." Mike knew that wasn't a real word the minute he said it, but it was true, they were glowing brighter.

"We need to get closer," said Jeff, standing far enough away with Shannon not to anger the T. rex.

"Wait," said Mike as he carefully approached the mother T. rex.

Dino-Mike put his hand up. As if the mother T. rex knew, she pushed the top of her head into Mike's hand.

"Okay," said Mike.

Jeff and Shannon slowly moved past the mother T. rex and behind Mike. Mike patted the mother on the head and then moved back to stand with Jeff and Shannon and the four young T. rex. The air crackled around them, and the T. rex glowed brighter.

"Now would be a good time to call your babies back, Samantha," said Mike to the mother T. rex.

The mother let out a snort and a low rumbling bellow. The four babies quickly left Mike's side and ran to their mother.

The air swirled around Mike, Shannon and Jeff.

"Thanks," said Mike to the mother T. rex.

Moments later, the group disappeared into thin air, leaving the four baby T. rex looking very confused.

Chapter 10

UNDERWATER AGAIN

"It worked!"

Mike didn't think he could be any happier to see Shannon's underwater home and dino sanctuary. They were standing in the time portal room, where Mike had made his journey to the past.

"Ha!" said Jeff! "Your plan worked perfectly, Mike!"

"I'm so pleased to be back home safely!" exclaimed Shannon.

"Your father knows we went, but will anyone else wonder where we've been?" asked Mike.

"Don't worry about *your* father. To him and everyone else, only a few minutes have gone by since we left," explained Shannon as they walked down the long corridor.

"That's a relief," said Mike. "I didn't get much information from your father about how this worked before I left."

Right on cue, Dr Broome and Mike's father walked round the corner.

"Son, where is your jacket?" said Mike's father.

"Oh, um, Dad, I think I…"

"Here's your jacket, Mike," said Dr Broome, holding a Dino Jacket. "You must have left it in the dock area."

Mike was confused. This couldn't be his jacket. The one his dad gave him was gone. *How is this possible?* he thought.

"Uh … thanks," was all he could muster.

"Interestingly," said Mike's dad. "Did I ever tell you that Dr Broome is, in fact, the person who designed the Dino Jacket?"

Mike was shocked. It all started to make sense. Dr Broome had filled the Dino Jacket with all those cool dinosaur-type gadgets. That's why Mike's father didn't know about so many of them.

"Wow. Thanks, Dr Broome!" Mike exclaimed.

"Not a problem, Mike. Just make sure you keep it in a safe place. I've put a few extra features in there for you to explore." Dr Broome smiled and winked at him.

Dr Broome then turned to Mike's dad and said, "You know something, Dr Evans? I like you, and I think we have a good working relationship. Plus the kids get on so well with each other. Would you consider working here with me?"

"I don't know what to say," said Mike's dad.

"Why don't we go back to my office and discuss it?" Dr Broome offered.

As the dads walked off, the children all stayed behind. Mike held the jacket out and stared at it. It was exactly like the other one. He wondered what new secrets were hidden inside. He couldn't help but smile.

Jeff stepped forwards. "I have to admit, you really helped us out, Mike. I want to apologize for all the horrible things I did. From now on, I'm going to do the right thing," he said. "Well, I better go and clean my room before I get into trouble again."

Jeff turned to go, but then looked back at Mike again.

"You're okay in my book, Dino-Mike, and you're welcome at our home any time," said Jurassic Jeff.

Mike smiled at Shannon. It had been a wild and crazy set of adventures from the minute he met both Shannon and Jeff, but he was pleased to have made such good friends.

"You seem happy," said Shannon. "Go on. Put the jacket on."

Mike put on the Dino Jacket. He pulled the hood with the T. rex face over his head.

ROOOOAAAAAAARRRR!

The familiar T. rex roar sounded and the bright lights of the eyes flashed on. It felt right.

Mike pulled the hood down. "I wonder if this one has all of the same gadgets as the last one."

"Knowing my dad, yes. All of them and probably a few you have yet to discover." Shannon laughed.

"This looks like a newer model," Shannon continued. "It probably has a portal key in there with a Return Remote. He's been working on perfecting how to control the time travel."

"Really?" said a shocked Mike. "Do you think so? Will I still be able to go to the Cretaceous period?"

"The portal doesn't just go to one time period," explained Shannon.

"So it can go anywhere in the past?" said an even more excited Mike.

"No ... not just the past. It can go ANYWHERE," she said.

"You mean –?" Mike began.

Shannon put her hands up in the air as if showing Mike the imaginary stars in the sky. "Do you remember the planetarium in New York? What if you could go to the moon or the stars, or better yet, to different planets … planets that aren't even in our solar system?"

Mike was stunned as he thought about her imaginary scenario. Shannon smiled and walked away.

Mike looked down at his Dino Jacket, and it began to glow slightly. A smile grew across his face.

Time for another adventure! thought Dino-Mike.

GLOSSARY

Jurassic period period of time about 200
to 144 million years ago

palaeontologist scientist who studies
extinct animals and plants and their fossils

pterodactyl prehistoric flying reptile
with large wings supported by very large
fourth fingers

triceratops large, plant-eating dinosaur
with three horns and a fan-shaped collar
of bone

tyrannosaurus large, meat-eating dinosaur
that walked on its hind legs, also known as
a T. rex

DINO FACTS!

What does the word "dinosaur" mean? The word comes from the Greek language and means "terrible lizard." In 1842, palaeontologist Richard Owen was the first person to call dinosaurs by this name.

The world's tallest dinosaur fossil is displayed at Museum für Naturkunde, Berlin's natural history museum. The Brachiosaurus is more than 12 metres high.

Tyrannosaurus rex lived between 65 to 145 million years ago during a time known as the Cretaceous period.

The T. rex's arms were surprisingly small. At only 90 centimetres long, they were too short to catch prey. Instead of grabbing prey with its tiny arms, T. rex grabbed food with its teeth. Each T. rex tooth measured more than 20 centimetres long!

T. rex used its giant teeth to satisfy a giant appetite. Scientists believe that with one bite the T. rex could gobble up about 200 kilograms of meat.

All of the T. rex fossils discovered have been found in North America. In 1990, one of the best-known and most complete skeletons was discovered in the state of South Dakota, USA, by fossil hunter Sue Hendrickson. The fossil, known simply as "Sue," is now on display at the Field Museum in Chicago, USA.

ABOUT THE AUTHOR

New York-born author and artist Franco Aureliani has been drawing comics since he could hold a crayon. Currently residing in upstate New York, USA, with his wife, Ivette, and son, Nicolas, he spends most of his days in his Batcave-like studio where he works on comic projects. In 1995, Franco founded Blindwolf Studios, an independent art studio where he and fellow creators can create children's comics. Franco is the creator, artist and author of Weirdsville, L'il Creeps and Eagle All Star, as well as the co-creator and author of Patrick the Wolf Boy.

Franco recently finished work on Superman Family Adventures, and is now co-writing the series The Green Team: Teen Trillionaires and Tiny Titans by DC Comics. When he's not writing and drawing, Franco teaches secondary school art.